This Book Belongs T

Still I Try

NIKKI ACE

ILLUSTRATED BY: Wesley Ace Jr. and Dani Ace

Book Series Theme:

PERSEVERANCE

One night a peacock, skunk, giraffe, chameleon ,wolf, and octopus got together for a **meeting** directed by a platypus.

Platypus is no stranger
being different from everyone.
He's like a mishmash of three animals
jumbled up all- in- one:

Flat bill, webbed feet
like you'd see on a duck,
paddle-shaped tail like a beaver . . .
and if that's not enough,
he has sleek fur like an otter
leaving you awestruck,
which is why he was the best
to lead this meeting and instruct.

He said, "Every single creature
has been **gifted** with a gift
that may look different from others,
but special qualities can't be missed.
You each have a special story,
so share with us your attempts
to prosper and propel
with your unique characteristics."

Skunk began the conversation
saying, "All the other skunks
make fun of me because
I can't **spray** funk coming out my rump!

When attacked, they all can spray
a smelly smell out of their rear end,
but when it comes to me
I have to be **creative** with my defense."

Skunk began to show his gift
he used against the hunter owl.
He stomped loud with a spine-chilling "HISSSSS!!!!"
so powerful, owl couldn't stand the sound .

Said the skunk, "I look like the others.
My abilities are not *all* the same.
This is not a sign of weakness *at all*.
My difference is my claim to fame . . .

I am matchless, one-of- a-kind,
the only *ME, ME, ME, ME, ME* . . .
I use my gift to flourish and thrive,
despite my difference . . .

. . . still I try."

Peacock shared a time
when he showed off his gift and strength.
Unlike the other peacock guys,
his tail has no beauty or glitz.

So to make the ladies like him,
he had to stand out when he'd compete.
He said, "I have the voice of an angel
and happy, groovy dancing feet . . .

So I started singing a tune 🎵
and all the ladies necks whipped.
Then I impressed them with dance moves -
I got so excited that I tripped.
I played it off like I did it on purpose
and ended my show in a split!
To say the least,
I was the winner
and I'm pretty certain it's because of my gift.

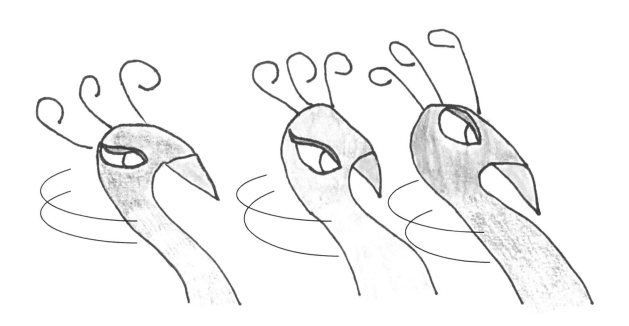

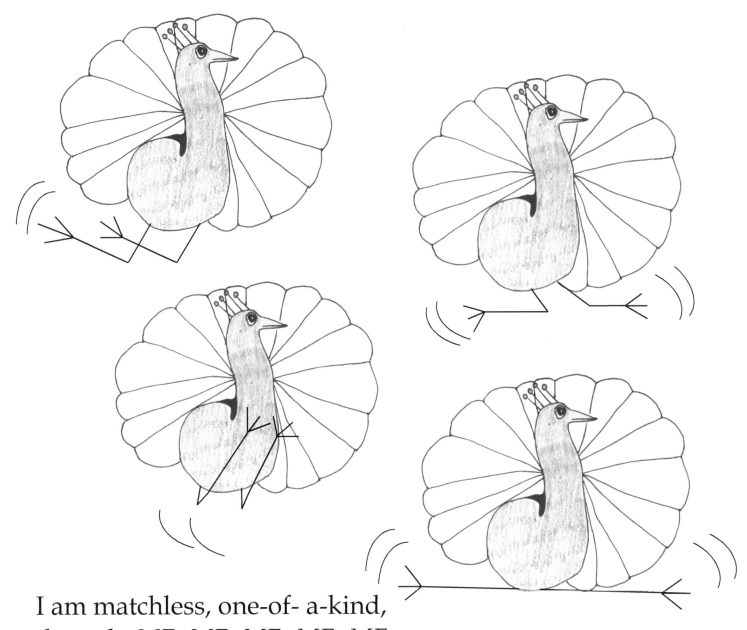

I am matchless, one-of- a-kind,
the only *ME, ME, ME, ME, ME* . . .
I use my gift to flourish and thrive,
despite my difference . . .

. . . still I try."

Wolves travel in groups called **packs**,
but this lone wolf was all alone.
No friends, no family, no one but him
or even a place to call his home.

"I was often lonely and in distress,"
said wolf and then he went in depth,
"but I used my fear as fuel
to help ignite the fire in my step!"
I became speedy fast as lightning -
as quick and swift as a sneaky snake.
No predator on earth could catch me
and you'd hate to be my prey. . .

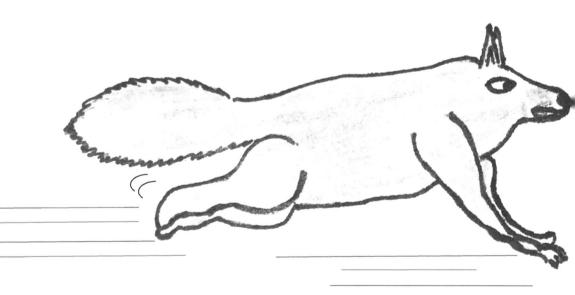

Although alone on a solo mission,
still I found my gifted strength
that may or may not had been discovered
without my i-n-d-e-p-e-n-d-e-n-c-e.

I am matchless, one-of- a-kind,
the only *ME, ME, ME, ME, ME* . . .
I use my gift to flourish and thrive,
despite my difference . . .

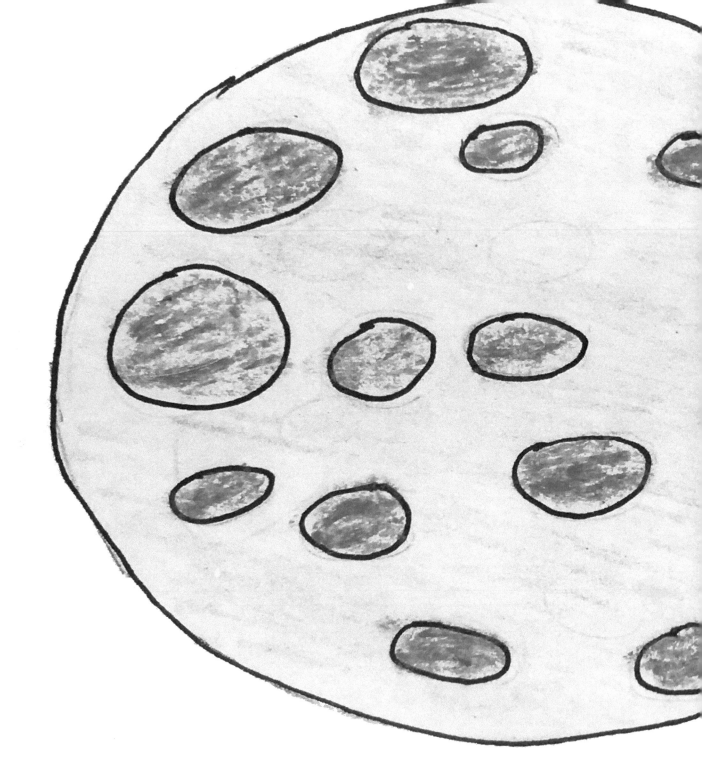

. . . still I try."

Giraffe chimes in and says,
"I want you all to look closely at me.

All other giraffes have necks like towers.
My neck is like a one-story building.

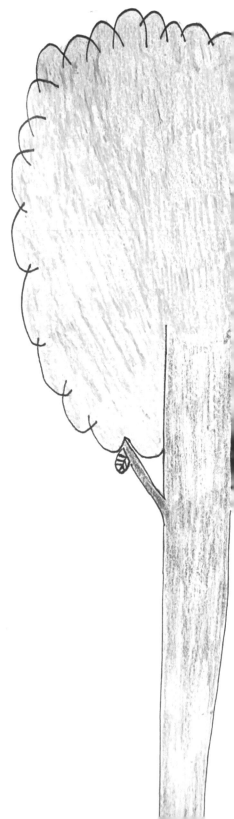

With little effort and energy,
they can reach the best twigs and leaves.
They munch on fruity deliciousness
from tall trees happily with ease.
However, my height won't allow me
to do what these other giraffes can do.
But I have a gift like no other,
my **SUPER JUMP** always sees me through!

Whether I hop or leap or bounce,
my vertical jump goes to outer space.
Although it takes more effort for me,
my **SUPER JUMP** is my saving grace.
I can reach the highest of trees
with just a jump that sends me flying!
It's quite a gift that I have -
there is no doubt . . . there's no denying.

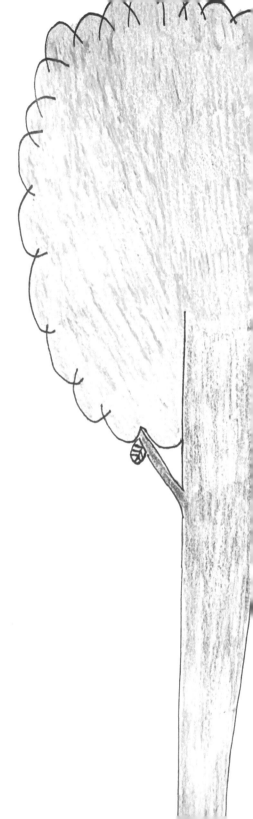

I am matchless, one-of- a-kind,
the only *ME, ME, ME, ME, ME* . . .
I use my gift to flourish and thrive,
despite my difference . . .

. . . still I try."

Chameleon is indeed, really easy to see.
Most chameleons BLEND INTO EVERYTHING!
However, she just isn't like *the most:*
She doesn't **camouflage**,
she shines bright head to toe.

"I wanted to dim my blazing light
and try to be like all the rest . . .
but I know I'm meant to stand out," she continued,
"shimmering **bright** is what I do best . . .

While others would hide and disappear -
I did the full complete opposite.
I'd put on display and demonstrate
my special gift by often modeling it.

I'm not always liked by other . . .
camouflaged chameleons
because my light just shines so bright
that often times it blinded them.

I am matchless, one-of- a-kind,
the only ME, ME, ME, ME, ME . . .
I use my gift to flourish and thrive,
despite my difference . . .

. . . still I try."

Octopus, with tears of joy,
couldn't contain her emotions **wholly**.
Happy, delightful, and full of bliss,
she couldn't wait to share her testimony.

She was proud to say,
"I have no suckers on any of my arms,
I use all eight arms to give great hugs -
no one will get stuck . . . no one will be harmed.

It's so sweet I can show the world
how I express my love and adoration!
Come here my friends! Let's shout it loud!
Let's sing our chant all over creation!"

"I am matchless, one-of- a-kind,
the only *ME, ME, ME, ME, ME* . . .
I use my gift to flourish and thrive,
despite my difference . . .

...still I try!"

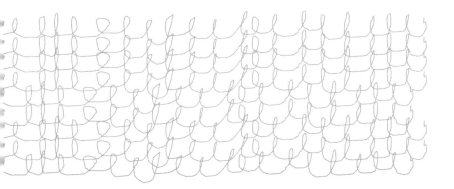

AUTHOR
(also colored most illustrations)

Nikki Ace

He's short. He's tall.
She's big. She's small.
He wins. He fails.
She can walk. She rides a wheelchair.
He's weak. He's strong.
She fits in. She doesn't "belong."
They see. They're blind.
For each, a **gift** is still assigned.

. . . .

Nikki Ace lives in Los Angeles, California with her lovely husband of 12 years – Wesley Ace – and their two amazing children – Wesley Ace Jr. and Dani Ace. She has authored *ten books* with the expectation of helping people understand the *beauty of God* and how He created each and every one of us in His incredible image.

ILLUSTRATORS

Wesley Ace Jr.
10 years old- Head Illustrator

Wesley's interests include baseball, playing the guitar, reading – history, realistic fiction, fantasy books - and making people laugh with his wit and charm.

Dani Ace
5 years old – Assistant Illustrator

Dani is fascinated by the beauty of horses, relishes in reading "girlie" books, and is extremely passionate about her singing and dancing.

This book is dedicated to every single person –big or small - that reads this book. You all have special gifts that are unique to you. Make sure that you use them!

To my best friend, my love, and my life partner - Wesley Ace - thank you for giving me the opportunity to fulfill what I believe God has purposed me to do. You have helped me to continue to reach toward my God-given potential and there is no one that I would rather flourish in life with. Incredible father and husband is an understatement – I'll simply call you a WINNER!
~With love always, Nikki

ALL RIGHTS RESERVED.

ISBN: 9781795150637
Library of Congress Control Number: 2019901829

"As each has received
A GIFT,
use it to serve one another."
-1 Peter 4:10-

CPSIA information can be obtained
at www.ICGtesting.com
Printed in the USA
BVHW061055271220
596468BV00014B/30